MW01227454

Strange
Friends

GARY LEE VINCENT

Burning Bulb
PUBLISHING

Strange Friends
By **Gary Lee Vincent**

Burning Bulb Publishing
P.O. Box 4721
Bridgeport, WV 26330-4721
United States of America
www.BurningBulbPublishing.com

PUBLISHER'S NOTE: This book is a work of fiction. Names, characters, places, and incidents are either the product of the author's imagination or are used fictitiously, and any resemblance to actual persons, living or dead, events, or locales is purely coincidental.

Copyright © 2020 Burning Bulb Publishing.
All rights reserved.

Cover concept by Gary Lee Vincent with photos from Michael Ochotorena, Tim Savage (Pexels) and Rakicevic Nenad (Pexels). Back cover photo by Brett Sayles (Pexels).

First Edition.

Paperback Edition ISBN: 978-1-948278-29-4

Printed in the United States of America

To Michael Ochotorena, who I met on
the set of *John Light* and who has enriched my life in
so many positive ways.

.

CHAPTER 1

The time was late evening on Friday night, and the Rooster Inn bar on Nogalas Highway was half full. The Rooster Inn wasn't yet completely submerged in a haze of cigarette smoke; that would come later, when it did fill up.

Nursing a whisky, Ross Blakely sat up by the bar counter, thinking grimly. Angry thoughts swam through his head like sharks.

"God will help you find my baby," his sister Samantha had said as he drove away from her house a little bit earlier. "I'm not gonna stop praying and God will surely help you find her."

Ross threw back his whiskey and laughed at that. "God will help me find the kid? Yeah right, and where was God when she ran away from home? Yeah, that I'd like to know."

"Huh, did ya say something?"

Ross looked at the man seated next to him, tall, Latino, half-drunk. "Huh?"

The man looked back at him through bleary eyes, his voice half-slurred by the booze he'd consumed; Ross had watched him knocking them back. "You said you wanted to know somethin'. Wonderin' what it was. See, I might know the answer."

Ross realized he'd spoken his thoughts aloud. "Forget it, man," he told the half-drunk guy, and then, before the guy could say anything else, he turned to the bartender. "Hey, Doreen, one more!"

Doreen Farmer was just setting down a beer in front of a guy at the far end of the bar. She looked up at Ross and nodded. "Coming up in a minute."

Ross and Doreen went way back, back to high school. They'd been friends since they were teenagers. Doreen was a large woman with long red hair, and a face well-scarred by life's battles. She owned the Rooster Inn bar.

Ross lived down the road from the Rooster Inn bar. He was a regular, in here most nights when he had nothing else doing. He looked around at the bar patrons: four 'redneck' guys in a booth near the front window, chugging beers and loudly discussing their recent fishing catches, raising their voices to be heard above the country and western music; a young woman he was certain he'd met before, who was looking nervous and constantly checking her wristwatch, and then lifting her phone to her ear and calling someone; some college kids getting drunk on tequila; another woman, a thin blonde whom Ross hadn't seen before. The blonde looked like she might be interesting to get to know. Ross was still trying to make up his mind on whether to go over and introduce himself to her, when the bar door opened and a stocky man with a beard entered.

The blonde immediately began smiling. Ross shrugged and waved to the stocky entrant—Tony Gassem, who owned the garage down the road. Tony waved back, then walked over and sat down beside the blonde. A waitress headed to their booth to take his order.

Ross forgot them both. He finished his drink.

"Another one?" a female voice asked.

He looked up at Doreen and shook his head. "Nah, I still gotta drive around town. Any more liquor and I'm certain to fail a Breathalyzer test."

She nodded understandingly. "Any luck with finding the kid yet?"

Ross shook his head. "None, but I've got my contacts working on it. Hopefully I'll get it wrapped up quick so I can get back to work." He frowned at Doreen. "You have any luck asking around with the snaps I sent you on Facebook?"

She shook her head. "Nothing for either version. Most people think she looks like a generic teen. They see lots of kids like that everyday, so 'cept they know her before from somewhere, she ain't gonna stand out."

Ross scowled at the reply. Doreen was right, of course; he hadn't actually expected much from sharing the pictures with her; but still, it had seemed worth a try. There was the faint possibility that someone might have noticed the kid somewhere.

"Hey, Doreen, how 'bout a beer over here, 'fore I die of thirst?"

"Coming, Sonny!" Doreen shrugged at Ross and walked off to served Sonny his beer.

Ross looked at his watch. A quarter of seven. Almost time to hit the road again. He was due to meet up with a guy named Broadway across town at seven thirty. The jukebox was playing some miserable Garth

Brooks tune, to which the man sitting beside him, the Latino guy who'd earlier thought Ross had been addressing him, was now singing along, while looking even more miserable than Garth Brooks sounded.

Behind the singing guy, a waitress was serving a laughing young couple a plate of hamburgers.

The young couple's happiness irritated Ross. It had been ages since he'd been happy like that. A lot of Ross's unhappiness was admittedly his own fault; but much of it wasn't. He wouldn't go so far as to blame God for his many woes, but thinking Fate had played some miserable tricks on him wouldn't be too far off either.

He looked back across the bar. Tony Gassem and his lady friend were both laughing too. Ross smirked.

That's just the old seduction trick. I know Tony like I know my own old shoes. Once he gets what he wants from her, he'll be gone ...

Ross once more forgot Tony and the blonde. *I've got serious business to attend to here.* He checked his watch. Like a snail in no hurry whatsoever, the minute hand was still inching its way towards seven.

Still too early to drive across town to see Broadway, and I don't wanna have another drink now, in case I need my wits about me tonight.

He looked up at Doreen. "A Coke, honey!"

The Coke arrived. To pass the time, Ross got out his phone and checked his call register. No one had yet called him; which could be both good and bad; either they were still looking for Jennifer or they hadn't found her. He took a sip of his coke and opened up the pictures of the kid in the phone's gallery.

For a moment, as Ross Blakely studied the two photographs of his missing niece, a tenderness filled him. In the first snap, Jennifer Wallace looked just how he remembered her—almost a carbon copy of her mother at that age—fifteen years old—dirty-blonde hair, blue eyes framed by large glasses and a nervous smile. Not really pretty, but not plain either. Jennifer was little bit on the heavy side, but that couldn't be helped, it ran in their family; both Ross and Samantha had been the same as teenagers. The kid was wearing a "The Real Rock Doesn't Roll" tee shirt and jeans, clutching a large blue Bible, and grinning at the camera. She was the image of cuteness.

The sight of the Bible made Ross smirk. A whole family of holy rollers.

But Ross's amusement evaporated when he swiped the screen and brought up the second picture of his niece, this one taken just two months ago. In this picture, fifteen year old Jennifer Wallace was already visibly in decline; already showing the signs of drug usage. Her face was drawn and haggard and she'd lost weight. Ross shook his head.

Yeah, when the good go bad, they really go bad, don't they?

He scowled at the picture, realizing what Doreen had meant by 'generic teen.' The cute glasses were gone and Jennifer had dyed her hair purple. Her "Rock Doesn't Roll" tee shirt had been replaced by one featuring some band that Ross had never heard of before; and if Jennifer's skirt had been even an inch shorter, her underwear would have been visible.

The girl also had a rebellious look in her eyes that Ross had never before associated with her. All of her cuteness had evaporated like steam, replaced by something very undesirable.

And this shot was taken when she was still living at home? What does she look like now? Tattoos and gauged ears?

Of course, Ross was judging anyone's looks. You looked how you looked. Lots of teens looked like this and it wasn't cause for concern. But when a mid-teen kid went from squeaky clean and big-time holy rolling to looking half-wasted in the course of two months, and then ran away from home to boot (and with her mum suspecting that she was shacked up with some guy), then alarm bells began ringing in Ross's head.

The look in Jennifer's eyes spoke of heavy drug use (her jacket hadn't let him notice if she had needle tracks on her arms) and he'd seen drugs destroy too many young people to let it happen in his own family too.

Apparently Samantha's pastor had been skeptical about the amount of difference in Jennifer after she'd stopped attending church and so Sam had taken the picture as evidence that she wasn't stretching the truth.

"Nice-lookin' kid," the half-drunk guy next to Ross said. "She your daughter?"

"Yeah." Ross nodded and closed the phone's photo gallery. Then, noting the time on the phone's screen, he added. "And I need to go pick the little hellcat up from summer camp."

The drunk guy nodded and took a swig of his beer. "You know, I've a daughter that age too. Sometimes she seems more trouble than she's worth; like I'd happily give her away for adoption. But if she ever ran away from home, I'd be totally devastated." For a moment he looked like he was about engaging Ross in a long conversation about the highs and lows of parenting a teen, but then another miserable country tune filled the bar and the guy began humming along with it.

Ross gestured Doreen over, paid his tab and left the bar.

CHAPTER 2

36-year-old Ross Blakely was a gangster. A mobster. Most times he worked with loan sharks. A guy owed you money and didn't want to pay? You called Ross and he went over there and had a talk with the debtor, a talk that might turn painful for the fellow if, say for instance, he had a big mouth and thought Ross was just bluffing about how he needed to pay up what he owed.

Ross hadn't had to kill anyone just yet, but he had broken more than a few arms and legs in the course of 'business.'

A hard, cold and suspicious man, Ross didn't think of himself as a nice person. To his mind, nice guys always finished last.

No, Ross agreed that he wasn't a 'nice' person. But he thought he was 'okay.' 'Okay' in that he did what was required to get along.

Was Ross selfish? He simply viewed it as 'looking out for number one.' To his mind, other guys always wanted what you had, be it money, a flashy car and luxurious house, or a beautiful woman. You had to keep eyes in the back of your head to avoid being backstabbed, and Ross wasn't adverse to doing some backstabbing of his own to get ahead in the mob world.

Now, driving away from the Rooster Inn bar in his Ford Mustang, Ross first stopped by his house to pick up his gun, and then once he'd gotten that, continued his trip to go see Bobby Miller aka Broadway.

Samantha's church, the Joy of Life Bible Church, stood about a quarter-mile from Ross's house. There appeared to be a service on tonight.

Ross smirked as he drove past the church. *Fools,* he thought.

Ross definitely didn't support his niece's running away from home, but he definitely agreed with her decision to boycott church.

He remembered one of his endless discussions with Samantha about this:

"All preachers do is fill your head with false ideas and ideals, until your head is so far stuck up in the clouds that you're no earthly good. Not to yourself, and definitely not to anyone else."

Samantha had sighed with that world-weary way she had that irritated him so much. "Listen, Ross, it isn't a con—God does love you. Jesus loves you. He loves you so much that he came to this world to die for you."

Back then—he'd been over at the Wallace's house for dinner that night—both young Jennifer and her father Donald had nodded in agreement when Samantha had spoken of God's and Jesus's love for Ross.

And now, barely two years later? Donald Wallace was dead—his car hit by a drunk driver who'd run a red light and rendered Sam a widow—and Jenny had turned druggie and run away from home.

So now, Ross felt justified as he smirked at the cars driving into the church yard. As he'd once mockingly asked his sister after Donald's death: "So, where's your Jesus when you need him, huh? Jesus seems to be like one of those 'good-time friends' who hang around you when you have money but who vanishes once you're broke. All God ever seems to do is make the faithful open their pockets so the preachers can enrich themselves."

And of course, Samantha had merely smiled pityingly at him, which had increased his anger, and he'd left her house, driven over to the Rooster Inn bar and gotten dead drunk.

Ross only went to church when people got married or were being buried, which in mob circles happened with quiet regularity.

But those fleeting visits to the house of God mere added to Ross's disinterest in things considered holy. Because Ross was certain that the majority of the gangsters buried in church cemeteries wouldn't ever be granted admission into Heaven.

He shrugged. "But still, well, if God won't find the kid for Sam, I'll do it for him."

CHAPTER 3

Bobby Miller aka Broadway, was a tall and thin man with a black goatee. Dressed in his regulation uniform of faded denim jacket and pants, Broadway regularly haunted the corner of Pike and 4th Streets, which was where Ross found him, chatting to some woman that Ross didn't know.

"Hey, man, what's up?" Broadway cheerily greeted as Ross pulled up beside him.

Ross leaned over and pushed the passenger door open. "Get in. Ain't got time to waste here."

Broadway at first looked like he was going to make some wisecrack or other, but then he clearly decided that Ross's face looked too serious for jokes, and merely nodded. He straightened up again and shrugged at his lady friend.

"Okay, later, Rochelle, gotta go handle some business."

The woman, a thin redhead, looked upset at the interruption. "Hey, man, you didn't tell me about this earlier. Are we still gonna go to the Roadhouse? I really wanna catch that new band I told you about."

"Hold on a minute while I check," Broadway told her, then he leaned into the car window and asked Ross, "How long is this gonna take?"

"How am I supposed to know that?" Ross growled at the man. "How long we spend talking depends on what you have for me."

Ross sighed when the man straightened up again. Broadway asking dumb questions like that might mean he was high. But he restrained his natural impulse to get out of the car and grab Broadway by his collar and drag him into the car. He waited patiently, taking deep breaths.

"So okay," Broadway told his female friend, "I should be back soon, but if for any reason I'm not, wait for me outside the Roadhouse with your girlfriends. But don't call me, I'll call you."

The woman walked off and Broadway got into the car beside Ross.

"You done fixing your love life?" Ross asked him grimly.

Broadway shrugged and ran his fingers through his oily hair." You know how it is, man. A dude's gotta hustle to survive." Broadway was twenty-five years old but looked thirty-eight; too much street living did that to a man. He had no actual job. 'Hustling' was what he did, a little bit of everything—most of it sordid—whatever would make him a little cash. Everyone knew him and told him things, and sometimes he could sell that information to others.

"So what have you got for me?" Ross asked. "You did make those enquiries like I asked you to? And don't tell me you forgot, 'cos if you did ..." Ross let the threat hang.

Broadway quickly shook his head. "Nah, man, I didn't forget." He knew very well what Ross for a living and was wary of getting on his bad side. And besides, with the amount of shady pies Broadway had his fingers in, it was very useful to have a tough-guy friend like Ross in the event that he got into some difficulties he couldn't handle. "Yeah, yeah, I asked around like you told me to."

"And...what did you find out?" Ross asked, parking his Mustang by the roadside.

"Well, I think the dude you're looking for is Joey Crockett."

Ross nodded slowly. "Name sounds familiar. Why's that?"

Broadway frowned. "You know Sloane Richards?" After Ross nodded, he went on: "Well, this kid Joey—he's about twenty...twenty-two years old—he used to work with Sloane. . But he either got greedy, or Sloane stiffed him in some deal they handled. Long story short, Joey left Sloane and went into the drug biz for himself. Pot, coke, horse, meth, Oxy, you want it, Joey can likely get it for ya. He's had one or two run-ins with the law, but they've so far been unable to pin anything on him."

Ross nodded. "Go on, I'm listening. How does this punk connect to the girl I'm looking for?"

Broadway nodded back at him. "Well, a junkie friend of mine told me that Crockett's got this teenaged girl living with him. Told the guy she's his sister, but the guy didn't buy it, you know? He said there was clearly something romantic going on between the two of them, even though the kid smelt like jailbait to him."

Ross could feel his breath quickening. "Did your friend describe the kid?"

"Yeah, he said she was about sixteen years old, about five foot four inches tall. Purple hair, blue eyes.

I showed him the Facebook pics of your niece and he said yeah, yeah, there was a likeness, but he'd been slightly high himself at the time and couldn't be certain if she was the same teen he'd seen. But really, according to the guy, Joey kept calling her Jenny anyway, so I figured she had to be your runaway niece."

Hearing this, Ross felt a deep anger building inside him. He scowled, then smiled coldly at his companion. You know where this punk Joey Crockett lives? I think it's about time that you and I paid him a visit."

Hearing that, Broadway quickly put up his hands like he was warding off evil. "Hey, hey, hey, man. I ain't going over there with you. You asked me to ask around for info, not to get my head shot off."

Ross laughed. "You're saying Joey's dangerous?"

Broadway nodded. "More like all those near drug busts are turning him paranoid. That's the thing. And using from his own stash doesn't help any; word on the street is that he's high half the time. On his bad moments, Joey's a lot like an itchy finger on the trigger of a loaded gun." He waved his hands again. "So, much as I like ya, Ross man, and I'll be glad to help you out any other way that I can, I ain't accompanying you over to that den of sin and iniquity."

Ross laughed again. "Den of sin and iniquity? That's what I'd expect my born-again sister Sam to say. You turning preacher too, man?"

Broadway laughed too. "It's just what my grandma used to say when describing dope joints."

Ross nodded. "Okay, I'll go alone. Where's the guy live?"

"A trailer over in Desert Village Trailer Park. You turn left after the old meat market and look for the turnoff on the right. Once you find that, just drive straight ahead till you reach Joey's hideout." He looked worriedly at Ross. "I'd advise you take some backup, man. The guy is paranoid, he's likely to shoot you on sight."

Ross laughed and pulled aside his suit jacket so Broadway could see the gun at his waist. "Don't worry, man. I got backup. I eat punks like that for breakfast and lunch."

Broadway nodded. "Well, it's your call." He checked his watch. "Hey, man, now that that's sorted out, how 'bout if you drop me off at the Roadhouse, so I can catch the concert with Rochelle. It's on your way to Joey's."

Ross nodded. "Sure, why not?" Before, he put the car in motion again, he got out his wallet and handed Broadway two hundred dollars. "Use this to treat your lady friend. You've earned it, dude."

CHAPTER 4

After dropping Broadway off at the Roadhouse, Ross called Samantha.

"Hello, Ross, did you find out anything yet?"

Ross slowed the car as he neared a red traffic light. "A guy I know says he might know where Jenny might be hiding. I'm headed over there now to check out his info."

When Sam spoke again, her delight and relief were evident in her voice. "Oh, thank God!" Then her voice turned worried. "Ross, maybe we should call the police now that you know where she is."

The traffic lights switched from red to green. Ross put the car in motion again. "Leave the cops outa this," he growled at his sister. "I already told you I'd handle it. I'm used to dealing with punks like this. I'll have Jenny back home in no time at all." Then, worried that she might call the police anyway and create a mess, he quickly added, "And besides, it's just a tip—the guy saw a kid somewhere who might be Jenny or might not be—It'd be dangerous having the cops bust the wrong guys."

"Okay, but be careful. And I'll be praying for you. God will be with you as you go."

"God? Sam, leave God out of this, will ya? Try to accept the truth here—God's left you in the lurch. He was never interested in your family in the first place and what's happening with Jenny now is simply proof that he never cared to begin with."

"But God told me to call you, Ross. When the police looked for Jenny and couldn't find her, my pastor and I prayed about it, and then God told me to call you and ask you to find her."

God told you to call me? Ross found that so funny that after hanging up he couldn't stop laughing all through the rest of his trip across town.

CHAPTER 5

Joey Crockett's place was easy to find. Once Ross made the turnoff Broadway had described, Joey's trailer stood out like a sore thumb. It was the only building visible for about a hundred yards of highway, with the next set of residences being a trailer park further down the road.

"Wow," Ross said aloud on sighting the trailer home, amazed at Joey's bravado at living so out in the open. "You'd think the punk would have more sense than to deal drugs from a place this obvious. Maybe Broadway was right in saying that Joey likes to get high on his own supply."

By now the sun was setting, the dusk settling into darkness. Ross drove up to the trailer and parked out front, next to another car, a white Chevy Malibu.

Ross saw no reason to conceal his arrival from Joey Crockett. The kid should have no reason to act crazy when someone announced his arrival upfront, when he looked out of his windows and saw that it wasn't the police.

Still, just in case ...

Before getting out of the car Ross pulled his gun from his waistband, put the safety off and pulled back the slide, though he made sure to keep the gun below the level of the dashboard before cocking it, in case Joey was watching from the house.

Ross replaced the gun in his waistband, buttoned up his jacket to conceal it, and then got out of the car. He wasn't really a fan of guns; he preferred to use his fists or something blunt but forceful like a baseball bat or a two-by-four. Guns were too dangerous; they did too much damage and in Ross's line of 'business,' where the aim was to 'persuade' the client to fulfill their 'contractual obligations,' shooting someone was mostly counterproductive, because if you killed them, then they couldn't pay their debts, could they? And even if you didn't kill them, a bullet wound was certain to have the cops giving you heat, and even if you could prove self-defense, you'd still be on the cop's books as someone who used a firearm and would very likely be pulled in for questioning the next time there was a shooting linked to someone who bore a resemblance to you.

So Ross avoided firearms as much as possible. A broken leg or arm (or the threat of one) generally worked much better in convincing someone to pay their debts or cough up protection money.

But in a case like this? Well, here the gun might be a lifesaver. If nothing else, assuming that Broadway's information was correct and that Jenny really was shacked up with Joey, the gun would convince the young man that Ross was serious about taking her home with him.

Ross shut the car door and walked up to the front door of the trailer. He knocked.

"Hey, Joey! Open up, I'm here to see you."

There was no vocal response, but Ross heard scrambling sounds from inside. Maybe someone had been having a drugged-out sleep and he'd startled that person awake. He resisted the urge to bang on the door, or try to force it open. Bad way to introduce oneself and if Joey got spooked enough, he could be setting himself up for a shotgun blast through the door. He looked down the road, towards the trailer park, and wondered how soon someone from there would respond to a shooting at Joey's place.

Then he knocked on the trailer door again. "Hey, Joey, I can hear you in there! I wanna talk to you!"

Finally a male voice spoke from behind the door. "Who's there?"

"My name is Ross. Ross Blakely. Open up, man. This is serious business."

The door swung open. Ross figured the kid standing there and staring at him had to be Joey Crockett. Joey looked like Broadway had described him, a druggy punk in his early twenties. He had long black hair, two or three tattoos and a lean and hungry face. He was barefoot and dressed in shorts and a Metallica tee shirt.

Ross was relieved to see that Joey wasn't armed.

"Hey, I don't know you, man," Joey said. "What're you here for? Man, if you're one of those undercover guys, don't even bother. I'm clean and my place is clean too, man." But Ross wasn't fooled. The young man's jerky motions, the way he seemingly couldn't stand still, gave away the fact that he was tripping on something.

Feeling he had an advantage, Ross shouldered Joey out of the way and stepped into the trailer home. "Don't worry your head about that, kid," he said as he stepped past Joey. "I ain't here about your recreational habits."

The interior of the trailer was sparsely furnished but very untidy, with empty beer cans and pizza boxes discarded everywhere, along with McDonalds hamburger wrappers. Joey Crockett clearly didn't take hygiene too seriously.

"Hey, man, you can't just come barging in here like that," Joey protested, then seemingly realizing that the protest was pointless, added, "So if you ain't the damn pigs, what you want here then? You wanna buy some dope, is that it?"

Ross turned and stared squarely at him. "I'm here 'cos I hear that you're keeping Jenny Wallace here with you."

Joey suddenly looked coy. "And what if I am? Who are you? Her father?" Then he shook his head. "No, you can't be her dad—she told me her dad's dead."

"I'm her uncle...and I'm here to take her back home where she belongs."

Joey's expression now turned dangerous, confirming to Ross that yes, Joey was sleeping with his niece. That didn't overly bother him though. "Okay, Joey, where is she?"

Joey laughed. "Who the hell do you think you are, man? Bursting in here and acting all tough like you own the town?"

Ross decided it was time to act tough. He grabbed Joey by the throat and slammed him against the living room wall. "I asked you a question, kid. Where is Jenny Wallace?"

Joey was having trouble breathing, but still managed to stutter: "Hey, man, she's passed out in the back room. She did too many Smartees and now isn't so smart. I left her alone to sleep it off."

Ross hit the kid with his free hand, a hard punch that drove all the air from Joey's lungs and left him wheezing for breath.

"She doesn't wanna go home," Joey sputtered weakly when he could speak again.

Ross shoved the young man away and shook his head in disgust. "Use your brains, you fool. She's not sixteen yet. The cops find her with you, it's statutory rape. Then what you think is gonna happen to you?" Then he shook his head. "But I guess with all that coke you snort you can't think too clearly anyway."

Joey looked about to leap up out of his seat and charge at him, so Ross undid his coat so Joey could see the gun. "Hey, stay calm and stay alive, boy. I just want my niece; it'd hurt me more than it does you to have to blow you away."

He glared at Joey, who didn't reply though he looked as dangerous as a tail-stomped rattlesnake, and then, figuring the young punk had gotten the message to calm himself down, strode off into the rear of the trailer to find his niece.

Jennifer was awake. Ross found her in the bathroom throwing up.

When Jennifer turned around Ross was shocked at the change in the girl. She was wearing a dirty pink halter top and shorts and it was instantly obvious she'd lost some weight. Not too much though, which was a relief. Ross had been worried that by the time

✦

he found Jennifer she might be emaciated—weigh ninety or one hundred pounds, half of what she had the last time he'd seen her.

And the expression on her face before she noticed him? While she staggered out of the bathroom with her eyes fixed on the floor? She looked like a lost soul, wiping vomit from her lips with the back of her hand and supporting herself with a hand on the trailer wall as she lurched towards the bed.

Seeing his niece like this, Ross felt a hatred for Joey Crockett so intense that he felt like he could kill him. It took him all of his self-control to not hurry back to the trailer's living room and fill the boy full of holes. Sure, Ross had met lots of drugged-out kids, but none of them had been related to him.

Jennifer finally noticed Ross. She stared at him in equal shock. "Uncle Ross? Uncle Ross, what are you doing here?"

"I'm here to take you back to your mom," Ross said coldly. "So gather up your things and let's go."

On hearing this, the worn-out look on Jennifer's face was instantly replaced by one of intense hatred.

"That hypocritical bitch!" Jennifer raged. "Forget it. I'm never going back to her. I'm staying here with Joey and Denny."

Denny? Who the hell is Denny? Ross wondered. *There's another kid living here with them?*

But he was so distracted by the way Jennifer looked that he pushed thoughts of this 'Denny' individual to the rear of his mind.

"Listen," he told Jennifer. "It doesn't matter that you don't like your mother—"

"I hate her! All she does is criticize my lifestyle! Ever since I stopped attending church all she ever did was tell me how much Jesus still loves me." She glared angrily at her uncle. "Yeah, if Jesus loved us so much, why'd he let daddy die like that, huh? Why didn't he let that drunk driver kill someone else; someone who actually deserved to die!?"

Ross was taken aback by the vehemence of her words. And it hurt him immensely to see how much hatred filled her sky blue eyes. "Well that's a question I've often asked myself," he replied her. "Why does God, if he's really a good God, let nasty people live and kill the nice ones? But I guess it's like the preachers all say—God works in mysterious ways." He looked closely at Jennifer, saw that she wasn't buying his stereotypical answer, and changed tactics.

"Well, it doesn't really matter if you wanna live with your mom or not, kiddo. Legally, you ain't old enough to live on your own yet, so I've gotta return you back home. Listen, while I sympathize with you that Sam can be hard to get along with sometimes, just endure it for—ungh!"

Ross had been about saying, "endure it for another two or three months until you're sixteen, when you can run away again, and I promise not to come looking for you then," but he didn't, because something hard next hit him on the back of his head.

Stunned, he found himself falling to hit the beer-stained bedroom rug.

Realizing that he'd been jumped from behind, Ross managed to remain on his hands and knees, but when he tried to reach his gun he was kicked in the side and the gun was taken away from him.

"Hey, wait!" he protested. "I just—"

But then another kick to the head knocked him out cold.

CHAPTER 6

Ross revived to a throbbing headache, a serious pain in his ribs, and the feel of cool breezes blowing over him. He smelt grass and dirt. Then he realized that he was tied up and his mouth was covered with duct tape.

Oh God no, he thought as fear flooded him. *How a simple intervention could go so wrong was beyond his comprehension. All I had to do was take Jenny home to her mother and now this happens to me?*

He had no idea how long he'd been unconscious for, but during that time he'd been moved outside Joey Crockett's trailer and was now lying somewhere in the woods; though this didn't seem to be the woods near Joey's home. Though it was fully night now, Ross made out a road somewhere beyond the wall of trees, with a car parked beside it. The car looked like his own Mustang But tellingly, there was no trailer near the car, and when he twisted his neck to look further down the road, he saw no sign of the neighboring trailer park either.

Joey, Jennifer and some huge guy who had to be 'Denny' were standing about twenty yards away from Ross, talking.

Ross's hands were bound behind him so that he couldn't reach his feet and free them, but he wondered if he could manage to roll away from the kids without being heard.

Ross had never felt this scared before in his life. He'd always been in control of situations, but this particular turn of events had snuck up on him so unawares that he was completely out of his depth.

Joey, Jennifer and Denny began walking in Ross's direction. A moment later, a flashlight was shone in his face.

"He's awake," Denny said, with some satisfaction. "I told you I wouldn't kill him, didn't I?"

"Might've been better if you had killed him," Joey retorted. "Now we gotta figure out what to do with him." He paused and ran the flashlight over Ross's body, then kicked Ross in the belly. "Hey, that's payback for the way you sucker-punched me earlier, tough guy."

The youths all laughed while Ross grunted in pain on the forest floor.

Joey's voice had a manic, drugged-up edge to it that marked him as being in a dangerous frame of mind. Ross watched the young man pull out a vial of cocaine from his jacket and use a key to snort some up. He wished they hadn't taped his mouth shut, then he could've pleaded with them to let him go; tell them that he'd tell Jenny's mother that he couldn't find her. And he'd keep his word too, tell Samantha that he didn't know where her daughter was. Because truly, Ross's credo had always been looking out for number one and there was no way that he considered the measly eighty or so days that remained till Jennifer Wallace reached the age of sixteen worth dying over.

But now his lips were sealed. Literally sealed.

Now, Jennifer was snorting cocaine, then she passed the vial and key to Denny. Joey was sniffing about like a dog that could smell danger or death in the air, Ross thought.

Denny passed the cocaine vial back to Joey, who took a final snort of the white powder then put it away again.

"Alright, guys," he said. "Now we gotta figure out what to do with Jenny's interfering uncle here."

"To hell with him, baby," Jennifer said in an icy voice. "Let's waste him."

"Yeah, I feel like killin' someone tonight," Denny said. The young man had a high-pitched voiced anyway, but the drugs had pitched it up into almost chipmunk range. "Yeah, c'mon, Joey, let's kill him. We can drop the body in that old pit out back. The one where we found the dead hog the other time."

"Yeah," Joey said. "Let's do it."

"Hmmph! Hmmph!" Ross grunted from behind his gag, thrashing desperately on the floor, struggling to let the kids realize that he was harmless to them; that he'd leave them in peace.

"Is he peeing himself yet?" Jennifer asked. "I hear that when people are really scared they start wetting themselves from fear."

She grabbed the flashlight from Joey and shone it in Ross eyes, then ran it down his body. "No, his pants are still dry."

"Yeah, once a tough guy, always a tough guy," Denny said. "Okay, so once he'd dead then we'll go have ourselves a party."

Jennifer walked back and hugged Joey, then she leaned up and kissed him. "Hey, baby, once he's dead, how 'bout we go visit my mom! It's about time she met her future son-in-law!"

"I don't think that's a good idea."

"Why not, baby?"

Joey burst out laughing. "Well, from what you told us 'bout your mom, she's no fun at all! We go over to your house and she'll most likely get out her Bible and start preaching at us."

All three of them burst out laughing.

Ross blinked and began praying in his mind. He didn't even realize that he was praying. *Oh, dear God, help me! Oh, dear God Almighty, help me now!* And as he prayed he suddenly understood how those he'd beaten up over the years had all felt when they saw the ruthless look in his eyes, and knew there would be no escape from the beating to come, that no matter what they did or said, Ross was going to hurt them.

Ross started crawling away, moving like a snake, rolling and humping his body across the leaves and roots in the way. Anything to flee these crazy kids.

"Ha ha ha ha!" Jenny laughed, pointing at him.

"Well at least he's heading in the right direction," Denny said. "Means we won't have to drag the corpse too far after we shoot him."

Ross kept moving, aware that his life was running out. *They're so jacked up, so spaced out, that they can't think straight. Jenny is even talking about taking Joey over to meet Sam, which can only result in another murder. God help me! God help me!*

Then Ross realized that his flight was pointless and simply gave up on it. As he crawled away the three kids were keeping pace with him, walking a few steps behind him and laughing, with Joey or Denny occasionally kicking him in the thighs or ribcage.

Fear in his heart, Ross turned over on his back and stared up at the three of them.

"Alright, let's get this over with," Joey said, pulling a gun from his pants pocket. "We're far enough away from town now that no-one'll hear the gunshot. And if we use his own gun, no one'll be able to trace it to us when they find him."

"And they won't find him for a long, long, time, right?" Jennifer asked.

"No they won't," Joey agreed. "Once he's in the pit, it might be years before anyone stumbles on his corpse."

"That was a great idea of yours to bring his car along too," Denny said. "The cops find it out there, there's really nothing to link him to us."

"Yeah," Joey agreed, "so long as we wipe it down for fingerprints before driving off."

"Where you gonna shoot him, baby?" Jennifer asked. Head or heart, or where?"

"Head's best," Denny said. "That way the guy doesn't suffer too much. And you're also certain that he's dead. If you shoot him in the chest you might miss the heart."

Jennifer bent over Ross. "Goodbye, Uncle Ross. Tell mommy's God that I hate him now. No, forget that...from what mom always told us about you, you're going to Hell for sure, not to Heaven."

And that was the exact moment when Ross realized that, yes, if he died right now, he was headed straight down to Hell; that he had zero chance of ascending skyward to be with the angels.

Now with the sort of life I've lived; not considering the kinds of things I've done to people. There's absolutely no way that God Almighty would have anything to do with me.

He'd have repented, but he had no idea how. Samantha always said that you just invited Jesus into your heart, but with his mouth taped over he couldn't do that.

Joey was already lowering the gun towards his head, and Ross was already counting the seconds till his eternal torment in Hell began, when he heard the words that gave him a fresh burst of hope:

"Hey, I think someone's coming," Jennifer said, in a worried whisper.

Joey instantly put the gun away again and hurried to her side. "Out here?"

"Yeah, listen."

With hope rising in Ross with each passing second, the three kids listened.

"Yeah, I can hear it too," Denny confirmed. "Hey, guys, let's scram."

"Aren't we gonna kill him anymore?" Jennifer asked in clear disappointment. "I'd really like to see what his brains look like."

"No, it's too dangerous," Joey said. "We don't know how many people are headed this way." He bent and kissed her. "Some other time, baby."

Next thing Ross knew, his niece Jennifer was peering down at him again. "Goodbye, Uncle Ross. Wow, I guess Jesus really loves you, even if he didn't love my daddy enough to stop him from dying."

Ross was brutally kicked and stomped a few more times and then the three of them melted away through the trees. A few moments later Ross heard loud footsteps approaching him.

Ross began weeping. He couldn't help it. The tears filled his eyes and ran from them in fluid torrents.

CHAPTER 7

"Good grief, man! What happened to you!?"

Ross's rescuer sounded like he was as young as his attackers.

"Help me," he gasped once the young man had peeled the duct tape away from his lips, and then once he'd been untied, let himself be lifted to his feet and more-or-less carried out of the woods.

At least one of the last salvo of kicks from the kids had hit Ross in the head. He was stunned and felt as helpless as a baby. He only came out of his daze when they reached the road he'd noticed from beneath the trees.

"Hey, there's my car," he told the young man, pointing down the road at it. "The kids brought it along to dump it here." There was blood in his mouth and speaking hurt but at least he could stand up unaided now. Being this beaten up really hurt his pride.

"Okay, we'll head over there," Ross's helper told him. "Hopefully, they left the keys in the ignition." He looked at Ross. "By the way, my name's Matt."

"I'm Ross, and thanks for rescuing me," Ross said and they made their way to the car.

"Don't mention it, man. It's just lucky that I happened on the scene in time. I was headed into town through these woods; there's a shortcut I take sometimes when I feel like hiking. But then I heard voices and decided to check what was going on. When I arrived I saw two dudes and a chick hurrying away from here. Those the guys who jumped you?"

"Yeah," Ross grunted, "and would you believe that the girl's my niece?" He spat blood on the grassy highway verge and then grimaced. *I still can't believe that Jenny was going to let that punk Joey shoot me. She was even egging him on. What the hell has gotten into the girl?*

"Your niece? And they beat you up like this? Did you attempt to molest her or something?"

Now, even though it was quite dark, Ross could see his rescuer Matt a little better. He was a tall young man, and seemed to have dark hair. "No, I didn't try to molest her," he grumbled. He felt he should say more to defend himself, but found that the effort of speaking was making him feel faint again.

"It's alright, dude," Matt said. "I believe you. Folks act all crazy nowadays. Particularly once they're high on drugs."

This kid looks like he's also about twenty years old, Ross thought. *Thank God he's on my side.* The irony of the fact that he wasn't just saying 'Thank God' in a casual sense, but actually meant it, escaped Ross.

They'd reached the car and Matt had gotten the door open. "Yeah, we're in luck. They left the keys in the ignition. Okay, time to get you to the ER."

"No, no hospital," Ross gasped, squeezing Matt's arm to emphasize his words. "I can't go to the hospital."

Matt helped him into the front passenger seat, then paused and stared at him. "Why not? Dude, you're all beaten up, you've got cuts on your face and you're bleeding—"

"No hospital. No cops!" Ross interrupted him. Going to hospital would mean the doctors filing a police report. The police would want to know what had happened, and he couldn't tell them Jennifer and her friends had done this to him. No, this was something he had to handle himself, in his own way.

I'm returning that silly girl home before she actually does kill someone!

He realized that Matt was still staring down at him, the kid's youngish face puzzled that Ross didn't want medical help.

"I mean it," Ross gasped, though breathing hurt like he might have a fractured rib. "I can't go to the hospital yet. Not for a few days, at least."

Matt finally shrugged. "Okay, it's your life, man, but if I were you, I'd definitely—"

"Just drive me home...please. Trust me, once I sleep this off, I'll be fine."

"Okay, where do you live?"

Ross told him the address. Matt shut the passenger side door, walked around to the other side and got in. He was about turning the key in the ignition when he paused and looked down into the driver's side foot well. Then he bent down and picked something up.

"Hey, dude, is this gun yours?"

Ross nodded across at him. "Yeah, the kids must've left it. I guess it was no use to them if they weren't gonna shoot me with it."

Matt nodded. "Crazy logic, but I guess anything's possible when you're high enough." He frowned at

Ross. "Okay, now I dig why you don't want to go to a hospital. Home it is then."

Ross was glad when Matt stopped talking and instead put the Mustang in motion.

Once the car was rolling through the night, headed for the West Side, Ross passed out.

CHAPTER 8

The next thing Ross knew, he was jerking awake again.

Thing is, he wasn't at home. He was lying in a bed somewhere, but it wasn't his own bed and this wasn't his own bedroom

His first worries, that Matt had panicked when he'd fainted and had driven him to a hospital despite his earlier protests to the contrary, were however wrong.

Because, sitting opposite him was Pastor Micah Princeton, the pastor of the Joy Of Life Bible Church, the church that his elder sister Samantha Wallace attended.

Ross quickly deduced that he was in the church parsonage. Staring out through the window beside his bed, he could see the highway, the same road he'd driven past the previous evening after leaving home, on his way to meet with Broadway, before the night's crazy events had unfolded. That must have happened 'the previous evening' because it was now morning again, meaning he'd been unconscious all night long.

"What am I doing here?" he asked Pastor Princeton. "I asked Matt to take me home."

The pastor, a balding man in his early sixties, got up and crossed the room and sat down beside Ross, who now realized that he'd been both cleaned up and patched up while he was unconscious. He had one bandage wrapped around his ribs and another one around his head and his shirt and jacket were both hanging in a closet across the room.

"You fainted in the car, and Matt decided to bring you to me instead," Pastor Princeton explained.

Ross nodded. Samantha had mentioned to him that her pastor had originally trained as a medical doctor, but had later retired from medical practice to become a preacher.

Pastor Princeton frowned. "You were lucky, Ross ..." He must've caught Ross's look of surprise because he then laughed. "Of course I know who you are. You're Samantha Wallace's younger brother, aren't you? Yes, we met at her husband's funeral." His smile turned sad. "Burying that godly brother was one of my saddest days since accepting to pastor this parish...but"—and now his smile returned, brighter than before—"but thank God Almighty that our brother Donald Wallace now resides in the bosom of the Lord Jesus Christ."

"You really believe that?" Ross asked, trying to sit up. This scenario—how convinced the pastor sounded—really bothered him. He was about saying more, but a sudden twinge of pain made him wince and grip his side instead.

"Easy, easy, man," Pastor Princeton cautioned, helping him to lie down again. "Matt told me about the gun in your car and how you didn't want to involve the police in what happened to you. Seeing as you're sister Samantha's brother I'll respect that, but...you should count yourself very lucky, Ross."

Ross laughed softly. "You don't know the half of it, preacher."

Pastor Princeton nodded. "Oh, I'm certain I don't. Now, listen to me for a minute." His facial expression now became that of a physician advising a patient. "Alright, Ross, your ribs are badly bruised but don't appear to be broken. And although from the way you're talking clearly right now, you don't appear to have a concussion, you really need to go in for a proper medical checkup to make certain of it, and also to have your ribs X-rayed. The best that I can do for you now is give you some painkillers that I've got here at home. Matt told me how he found you—"

"How do you know Matt?" Ross asked. "Is he a member of this parish?"

Pastor Princeton shook his head sadly. "No he isn't. Brother Matt just does some volunteer work for us from time to time. He's a dedicated Christian, that's for sure and I'd love to have him here for good—he'd make a fantastic youth leader—but he's also got wanderlust of the worst kind."

"Wanderlust?" Ross was intrigued.

The pastor nodded. "Yes, brother Matt seems to find it unable to remain long enough in any one place to put down roots. He's always travelling around the country, doing odd jobs to pay his way, though from the few discussions that I've had with him, he's very highly educated and could easily make a good executive somewhere." He shook his head. "Strange thing to find in a Christian, but then, God has all kinds of children. Take last night, for instance. Once Matt had helped me carry you inside here, he ran off again, saying he was late for an appointment with a friend."

"I owe him my life," Ross said. "If he hadn't come by, Jenny and her friends would have killed me. There's no doubt in my mind about that. They ran off when they heard Matt coming."

The pastor nodded solemnly. "Yes, Matt told me about that. Well, I guess I should be relieved to hear that young Jenny Wallace is still alive, though it's time that she rededicated her life to Christ and returned to the Lord's fold again...before something truly terrible happens to her."

Ross couldn't agree more with that. After the night's harrowing experience, a mental picture of Jenny sitting beside her mother on a church pew wasn't such a bad image anymore. In fact it was something that Ross now considered highly desirable. *She's not yet sixteen and wants to watch someone being killed?*

"She's already doing drugs," he muttered helplessly.

"Too many teenagers are these days. If we had more of Jesus in our high schools instead of ..."

Pastor Princeton fell silent, then said: "But, Ross, you're wrong about one very important thing."

"Yeah, what's that?"

"Well, you just said you owed Matt your life. You're wrong there, God and God alone is the reason you're still alive."

Ross made a face like he'd just swallowed a bitter pill. "God?"

The pastor nodded. "Yes, God. Matt was merely the instrument that God used to rescue you. Brother

Matt's being at the right place at the right time was simply God at work, and my God is never late."

Ross scowled skeptically. "So you're saying God kept me alive tonight?"

The pastor beamed broadly. "Of course, he did."

"But why would he do that? Why would God and Jesus let Jenny's father Donald die—and he was a church member and a good Christian and all that—and yet save me, who ain't been to church in ..." he shrugged, "well, only God knows how many years."

Pastor Princeton was still smiling. "Well, sir, our Lord does work in mysterious ways and one must never presume to interpret his divine reasons...but if you ask me, I'd say it was partly because Don Wallace was born again and as such went to Heaven when he died, while you—and your sister has told me a little bit about your *job*—aren't yet saved and would have gone straight down to Hell if you'd died tonight."

The pastor stopped speaking, as if giving Ross time to consider this. And Ross did consider it. Previously, Ross would have shrugged off all this talk of hellfire and brimstone, but not tonight. Now, as he considered the pastor's take on why 'God' had 'saved him' tonight, he didn't doubt the truth of it. He did his best to doubt it, but it didn't work—no matter how hard he tried, he couldn't forget that moment when, certain that he'd shortly be dead, the deep conviction of his eternal and irreversible damnation had smacked him in the face like a sledgehammer.

"Dude, you're right," he finally admitted with a sad smile. "At the moment when I thought I was going to die, when I'd known for certain that nothing in this world could possibly stop those young punks from shooting me in the head, I'd known, with a deep intuition, that the Devil was waiting for me down below with a broad grin on his face."

He fell silent. Barely three hours ago, he'd have felt silly admitting what he'd just told Pastor Princeton. But that was then, and this was now.

At the moment, Ross felt like he was standing on the edge of a precipice, staring down into the abyss. He was teetering, knowing a fall was inevitable, but would he fall forward or backwards? That was the question he couldn't answer. He realized that his understanding of his final destination if he died at this very moment meant that he needed to take an action of some kind, but he was unsure what that action would be.

He realized that Pastor Princeton was watching him with a thoughtful look on his face.

"Man, that was really heavy, you know?" Ross told the pastor. "To know that if I died I was heading down to the fire?"

"Thankfully, you don't have to take that ride, Ross."

"Huh?"

"Yes, yes, I know. You've heard it all before and you didn't believe it. But it's true, Jesus Christ the son of God did die for your sins and mine, and accepting him as your lord and personal savior is really the only way to keep from going to Hell after you die."

Ross said nothing, still hedging, trying to back out of something that seemed inevitable. *It looks like I'm about to fall over the precipice anyway. But forward or backward? Is my life about to get better, or worse?*

Pastor Princeton nodded solemnly at him. "Well, Ross, I think it's decision time. And from the expression on your face I'd say you know that too. So, what's it gonna be, my friend? Will you accept Jesus into your life as your lord and savior, or will you reject him once more like you've done so many times in the past...and leave here knowing for certain that you're still Hell-bound once you die?"

Ross felt a cold fear creep over him; and the memory of how close he'd been to not having this opportunity to repent. Feeling lost at sea, hopeless and helpless, he stared up at the pastor.

"Hell no, man," he replied. "How do I get saved? I mean for real?"

Pastor Princeton smiled. "It's simple. Just repeat this prayer after me....Lord Jesus, I come to you now as a sinner. I repent of my sins and ask that you cleanse me of them by your precious blood that you shed on the Cross of Calvary. I submit my life wholly to you and ask you to come into my life and be my Lord and savior. Amen."

Ross repeated the words after the pastor, with solemnness and honesty. While praying he had no idea what to expect, but was surprised at the instant change he felt inside of himself.

All he could do was stare at Pastor Princeton in wonder.

"I...I feel as if the world's greatest burden has just been lifted off of my shoulders," he gasped. "I feel so light...but most of all, I just feel so clean...clean...so CLEAN!"

The pastor smiled back at him. "Yes, it's done, brother Ross. Welcome into the fold of our Lord Jesus Christ."

CHAPTER 9

Samantha Wallace arrived at the parsonage about ten minutes later.

Pastor Princeton had phoned her after patching Ross up last night, had assured her that her brother was alright, and then asked her to come over to the church in the morning.

She was scared by the sight of her brother, and terrified by the news of what had happened to him and what was happening to her daughter (though Ross thoughtfully left out any mention of Jennifer's involvement in the attempt to kill him).

But she was utterly delighted when Pastor Princeton informed her that Ross had now accepted Jesus as his savior.

"Your brother is now born again and on his way to Heaven," the pastor said.

"Oh, praise the Lord!" she yelped and leapt on Ross and hugged him so tight that he was certain she was bruising his ribs all over again.

When she finally let go of Ross, he saw that she was crying. "Oh, my dear Lord, I'm so so so happy!" she wept, the tears rolling down her cheeks. "I've prayed so long for you to see the light. And after Donald died, it looked like it would never happen. Oh, dear God thank you, thank you so much!"

Then she sat down beside his bed and held his hand.

Ross stared warmly at her. He felt so different now that it was almost impossible to explain it to himself. But most of all he felt safe, certain that if he died right now, if someone shot him right now, he was going to Heaven and not Hell. He couldn't explain how he knew he was Heaven-bound now, but the knowledge resided somewhere inside of him, and it was a knowledge that he knew no one would ever be able to take from him.

***

"But what are we going to do about Jenny?" Samantha asked. "We need to get her back, both home and into church again, before something really evil happens to her." She looked at the pastor, still pleased that her brother had become a Christian, but also very worried for her daughter's wellbeing and safety.

The pastor looked from her to her brother. "I think that now that we know where she's hiding, we really should call the police and let them handle this."

Ross quickly shook his head. "No, you don't wanna handle it like that."

"I don't understand why we shouldn't," Samantha said. "I think Pastor Princeton is right—the police are best equipped to get Jenny back for us."

Ross nodded. "Well, in theory calling Child Services and the police is the right approach—the sensible thing to do—but in practice, well, too much could go wrong. The crew that she's hanging out with—Joey and Denny—those two youths are killers, real wolves—they showed me their teeth tonight, but God foiled them, praise the Lord."

Ross was surprised by how easily that "Praise the Lord" had come to his lips. He hadn't consciously thought of it, that was for sure. It had just seemed to be the correct thing to say.

He went on: "Thing is, if we tell the police where Jenny is, they'll definitely go to get her, but there's no guarantee that they'll retrieve her from there unharmed. Trust me, jacked up on cocaine like those three were tonight? They'll think nothing of taking on the cops in a gun battle, and then what happens? So, not the police, we want Jenny back alive, not dead."

Samantha instantly burst out in tears. "Oh, my poor baby girl, taking cocaine and shooting at the police? Oh, dear God, please, she's just a little kid! Help me get her back alive and well!"

"Calm down, sister," the pastor said soothingly. "I believe that our lord God Almighty is already at work in this situation,"—he nodded at Ross—"which I believe is why he had you call your brother in the first place. And see what's already happened: In just three days, brother Ross has located Jenny, something that the police had been unable to do for a month." He smiled. "So have faith, sister. God is on the case, and he neither leaves nor forsakes his own."

Samantha calmed down and wiped her eyes try with a tissue from her purse. Then she looked at Ross. "So what are we going to do then?"

Pastor Princeton nodded at Ross. "Yes, brother, what steps do you advise that we take?"

Ross frowned at them. "Just leave it to me. I'll bring her back home to you." He'd been trying to sit up, but the effort proved too much for him and he winced with pain, which made him quickly add: "Just not for the next two or three days, I need to heal up."

"But you can't," Samantha protested. "It's too dangerous."

Ross nodded. "Yeah, maybe. But like the pastor said, God involved me in this for a purpose. And if he kept those two guys from killing me tonight...then I suspect I'll be okay next time too."

"Well, we'll both pray along with you," Pastor Princeton said. "I don't know why, but I also believe our Lord has a hand in what's going on with Jennifer now."

Samantha nodded. "Okay, pastor, I guess I'd better take Ross home with me now. I can't let him go back to his own place in his current condition."

And unlike before, Ross now actually looked forward to going home with her. For one thing, his mind was already bubbling over with questions about scripture that he wanted to ask Samantha.

But first, he had a question for the pastor: "Do you have Matt's cell number? I wanna give the kid a call; thank him for helping me out tonight. Yeah, God surely used him—without Matt I'd have been a goner."

But Pastor Princeton shook his head. "Sorry, but I don't, Ross. Matt's always losing his phone. It's either that or he's forgotten it in whichever town he last visited."

"So how do I contact the kid?" Ross asked. "I'd really like to say thanks to him."

The pastor thought a bit. "You can leave your phone number with me and I'll ask him to call you when next he comes around; which might be as soon as tomorrow as he's sure to be curious about how you're doing"—he grinned—"well, so long as he hasn't gone on some overnight trip out of state again."

Ross grinned back. Yes, despite his injuries he felt right as rain.

CHAPTER 10

Bobby Miller aka 'Broadway' had been watching Joey Crockett's trailer for a whole day and a half now.

Ross had called him yesterday morning and offered him five hundred dollars to keep an eye on Joey and the girl for him. That was good money, not the kind of money that Broadway was going to turn down except for a very good reason.

So he'd bought some packed sandwiches and ridden his motorbike over to the woods near Joey's place. He'd been watching the trailer since then. But so far, no show; neither Joey nor the girl had come home since.

He'd reported back to Ross on this. "Looks like nobody's home, man."

"Anyone shown up to buy some stuff off of them? That other guy Denny might've taken the car off to do some business ..."

"Nah, man, no one's been over here all day. And I don't think anyone's in the trailer either. The lights didn't even flicker on last night."

"Keep watching," Ross had replied. "They gotta come back some time. All I gotta know is that my niece Jenny is still with them, that's all."

"Yeah, sure thing, man. You're the boss."

To Broadway, the odd thing here wasn't the job that Ross had hired him to do. Rather, it was the fact that each time he spoke to Ross on the phone, the guy sounded happy, like he'd fallen in love or something, which might also explain the reason why he apparently didn't have the time to show up and watch Joey's place himself.

He also sounded *nice*, nothing like the Ross that Broadway knew and dreaded.

Nah, the guy sounds almost human now. And that's more scary than Joey Crockett on speed.

So Broadway had kept the place under surveillance. He was in a safe spot, and his motorbike was black in color, meaning there was no way Joey would ever see him from his trailer, but, even with a constant flow of heavy metal music from his headphones and Netflix for company, the constant watching was getting boring. His behind had begun hurting from sitting in one place with his back to an elm tree and each time he heard the grass rustle around him, he gave a start because he was scared of poisonous snakes.

As agreed, he called Ross back every three hours or so.

"Nothing to report, man."

The reply was always the same. "Keep watching. A chicken's gotta come home to roost sometime."

But Broadway already had the deep feeling that something was wrong somewhere. With the kind of business Joey Crockett reputedly did now, his trailer should be overflowing with folks dropping by to buy drugs off of him.

But nothing. So finally, when it was getting towards evening, Broadway had no choice but to ride his bike back into town to go shop for more food so he'd have enough to tide him through the night watch.

He saw no danger in leaving his vantage point. If Joey hadn't shown up till now, he was unlikely to be in such a hurry when he did show up that he'd leave home before Broadway returned from loading up on beer and chips and more sandwiches.

And fortuitously, it was while buying beer at the Mini-Mart that Broadway saw Joey's white Malibu roll past the store, with Joey riding shotgun in front while Denny drove; and of course, Ross's purple-haired niece sitting in the backseat.

Only thing was, Denny wasn't heading home as expected, but rather away from it. And he had his phone to his ear and was laughing like he was making a business connection with someone.

But Broadway was with the Mini-Mart's cashier then and by the time he'd gotten done paying for his purchases, Joey's car was long gone. But by now he had an idea of what to do.

Once he'd loaded up his groceries on his bike, Broadway placed a call to the friend who'd initially told him he'd seen Jenny in Joey's trailer.

"Hey, Craig baby, what's up?...Man, I'm trying to get ahold of Joey Crockett?...Some dude I know from out of state wants to buy a load of blow from him?...Yeah, but when I drove out to his place he wasn't there. Trailer looks empty....He's what? ..."

Broadway listened. The story was simple: Apparently, Joey had gotten scared that the cops would be after him for some reason and had moved from his house; two midnights ago, he'd packed up his drugs and his jailbait girlfriend and scrammed.

Meaning that the trailer Broadway had been watching for the past two days had been abandoned all along. According to Craig, Joey was still in town and still dealing, but no one knew where he now lived.

"Thanks, dude," Broadway said and hung up. Then frowning, he put his motorbike in gear and headed back over to Joey Crocket's supposedly abandoned trailer.

Because Broadway still had to confirm what he'd heard. Nice-sounding as Ross Blakely was now; Broadway knew he'd be very angry indeed if Craig's info turned out to be wrong. Angry enough to break Broadway's legs even.

But Craig had been right. When Broadway reached the trailer, it was empty. The front door wasn't even locked. Broadway walked in and looked around. The obvious sign that everyone had moved house was the lack of any clothes in the place. The drawers and closets were all empty and there was an open suitcase on the bedroom bed.

Broadway took all of this in and then, wondering if Ross would still pay him after this, he sat down on the stripped bed, pulled out his phone and dialed the man.

"Hey, man, I got some bad news for ya ..."

CHAPTER 11

"Yeah, sure thing, I'll still pay you, man. Thanks for watching....And hey—Broadway...keep your eyes and ears open in case you get a lead on them."

Ross hung up, walked away from the bedroom window, and sat on the bed again. *Joey's no longer living in the trailer?*

Ross figured the news wasn't entirely unexpected. When you leave a tied-up and bleeding man lying in the woods, you certainly should expect a visit from the police.

Confused as to what his next move would be now, Ross changed from his bathrobe into some proper clothes, and then went downstairs to tell Samantha the bad news.

***

The past two days had been a wonderful surprise for Ross. Being a Christian turned out to be everything the 'holy rollers' had claimed it was. Ross couldn't get over how different he felt. Not externally, of course...but he had a joy and a peace he'd never felt before. And he also felt an intense love for God that was impossible to explain.

Each time he tried to explain it to Samantha, she just nodded. "That's what I've been trying to tell you for years. That's the peace of God. That peace is how

I've managed to cope with Donald's death, and how I'm managing to cope with Jennifer's running away. God...Jesus said that he'd never leave nor forsake us. And I take him at his word."

Ross understood that now. Samantha had given him her late husband's Bible and he'd been reading through the book of John, for the first time really understanding that the life of Jesus wasn't just a fable, but something that had actually happened, that God really had cared so much for this sinful world that he'd sent his only son to die for it.

Ross had been praying too, and while he wasn't sure he was praying right, each time he knelt by his bedside, he did have the assurance that he wasn't just speaking to the air.

"God, please help me find Jenny again," he prayed silently now. "I need to bring the child back home safely."

The past two days had also helped heal his body. He still felt pain while moving, but he was able to get around unaided.

He felt ready to resume the search for Jennifer. He just didn't know where to look.

***

Samantha took the news that Joey had moved house better than Ross had expected.

Ross could see that she was holding back tears, but she nodded and calmly said, "I believe that God is still in control of the situation. I think we should visit the pastor and have him pray with us about it."

And so that's what they did. After Samantha called to confirm that Pastor Princeton would be available to receive them, they set out for the church.

***

Pastor Princeton welcomed them both with open arms. After warmly hugging Ross he listened to their update on what had happened. "Yes, you're right, my dear brother and sister, in a situation like this one, prayer is the only thing we can do. God's eyes and ears are everywhere, all over the earth. He knows where young Jennifer is right now and he will help us find her." He nodded at them. "Let's pray."

They bowed their heads where they sat and the pastor led them in a word of prayer: "Dear God, please help us find this missing child Jennifer Wallace, who is also one of your children though now she is backslidden. Almighty God, please help us bring her back safe and sound to her family, oh Lord. And Heavenly Father, please also return her to your flock. Clear the Devil's deceit from her young eyes, so that she may see the error of her ways and return to seek your forgiveness. In Jesus' name we pray."

"Amen," Ross and Samantha both chorused.

"So what do I do now?" Ross asked the pastor.

Pastor Princeton tapped his fingers on his desk. "Now, brother Ross, we wait for God to answer our prayer. No, I don't mean that you don't do anything. But I trust that God will lead you in the steps you will take to find Jenny. Relax and thank him for leading you."

Pastor Princeton had a previously-scheduled appointment then and so Ross and Samantha had to leave. But just before they exited the pastor's office, Ross asked him, "Has Matt been in contact with you yet?"

The pastor nodded. "Yes, he has. He came here yesterday. I gave him your message. He was utterly delighted to hear that you were now born again, and he promised to drop by sister Samantha's house to see you."

"We haven't seen him," Samantha said.

Pastor Princeton laughed. "Oh, you know how that young man is. He probably got sidetracked into doing something else. Don't worry, brother Ross. I already conveyed your gratitude to him and I'm sure he'll stop by to see you once he has the time. And brother Ross ..."

"Yes, pastor?"

"While searching for your niece, please always remember this scripture: 'God will give His angels charge over you, to keep you in all you ways; they will bear you up in their hands, lest you hit your feet against a stone.' That's from Psalm 91, verses 11 and 12." The pastor smiled at them both. "Always remember this promise of God's—that His divine angels are watching over you."

CHAPTER 12

Ross drove himself and Samantha back home. Though he'd intended to immediately drive into town again to resume his search, the trip to see the pastor had tired him out and he wound up falling asleep instead. Sam woke him up to eat lunch and then he fell asleep again.

That evening, as the sun began to set, Ross decided to head over to Joey Crockett's abandoned trailer. He felt refreshed enough now.

With no other leads to follow for the moment, Ross figured he'd search through the trailer for any clues he could find, anything that might indicate where the trio had relocated to.

He took his gun with him. He didn't want to shoot anyone but he wasn't about letting himself be jumped from behind and tied up again like had happened to him the last time out.

Almost as if balancing out the threat of violence with one of his new salvation, he also took along his Bible.

Arriving at the trailer, Ross thoughts were a strange mix of pleased and troubled. *At least—according to Broadway's info—we know they're all still in town. It would be real hard if, for instance, they'd moved down to Tucson.*

He parked the car by the trailer, got out, and gun in hand but concealed beneath his jacket in case a police cruiser was driving by, hurried over to the front door and pushed it open. After waiting to make sure no one was home, he put the gun away and shut the door.

Okay, it's time to search. Oh, my dear God, what a mess this place is! Sure, it was a mess before, but now it's twice as messy.

He took his time with the search, silently and patiently rifling through drawers and closets for almost an hour, but found nothing.

Then, as he sat on the dirty living room couch wondering what his next step should be, a voice called out to him from outside the trailer. "Hey, Ross, are you in there?"

Ross pulled out his gun before replying. "Yeah, man, I'm in here. Who is it?"

"It's Matt!"

Both relieved and surprised, Ross quickly put the gun away and hurried to the trailer door.

Yes it was Matt out there, sitting on the hood of his car.

And now that it was daylight and he wasn't half-stunned, Ross got a proper look at his rescuer. Matt looked to be about twenty-four years old, was about six feet tall and had long brown hair and smiling blue eyes. Physically he was very muscular, which Ross figured came from all the traveling he did, all the odd jobs he worked to pay his way. He was wearing jeans, boots, and a blue tee shirt with "Jesus Saves" printed on it.

"Really glad to see you, man," Ross said, walking over and shaking his hand.

"Glad to see you too, dude," Matt replied. "And yeah, you're looking much better than the other night in the woods."

Ross laughed at that. "Yeah. Thanks for helping me back then, man. If you hadn't come along then, I'd have been a goner for sure."

Matt laughed. "Thank God, man. The Lord is watching out for all of us. Hey, the pastor told me you got saved. How's that feel?"

Ross shrugged and also sat on the car's hood. "Feels real strange, but I'm getting used to it." He laughed. "I think I'm doing okay with the Bible-reading, but the praying aspect still has me stumped."

"Prayer's easy, man. You just talk to God and expect him to reply. Just like speaking to anyone else you know. You've just gotta remember to pray in Jesus' name."

"Yeah, I think I can ..." Ross stopped and stared curiously at Matt. "But, hey, what're *you* doing over here?"

"Oh, I dropped by your sister's place to see you, but she said you were over here. So I thought I'd come by to see you."

Ross nodded at that; he'd told Samantha he was going to take a look at the trailer. But then he had another question: "Yeah, man, but how did you know where Joey's trailer is? Or did I mention it to you the other night when I got beaten up?"

Matt grinned and waved the question aside. "Forget that for the moment—an explanation would take too long. The important thing now is that while you've been healing, I've been keeping an eye on Joey Crockett for you. I know where he lives now."

Ross's heart began pounding with anticipation. "You do?" *Wow, it looks like God really does answer prayers!* he thought. That realization was a real surprise to him

"Yeah," Matt replied. "That's why I went to sister Sam's place looking for you, so we could head over to Joey's together."

Ross saw no sign of Matt's own transport, so he figured he'd either hitched a ride from someone, or called a Uber.

"But why are you so interested?" he asked. "What's your concern in this?"

"Let's just say I've got personal reasons for getting involved," Matt replied with a grim look on his face. "Punks like Joey Crockett really annoy me. The drugs they deal corrupt lots of young lives. For instance, look what he did to your niece. Turning a decent Christian girl into a slut and a tramp! I knew Jenny when she attended our church—she was a good kid with promise, wanted to go to law school. And now that she's hooked up with Joey Crockett? Well, half the time now Jenny can't tell which way is up...and she's not the only kid Joey and Denny have messed up like that. So I figured it's time someone staged an intervention for Jenny. And seeing as you wanna do that, I'm with you all the way."

Ross winced at the truth of Matt's words, but yet still couldn't help looking at him with some suspicion. "Hey, you seem to know a hell of a lot about Joey's business."

Matt shrugged. "I get around, keep my ears to the ground. It's just that this time, my business and his business have gotten entwined." He pointed to the sky. "Man, it's dark now. Let's just head over there and get Jenny and leave."

Ross shook his head. "Hang on a sec. We gotta be careful here—those punks are crazy. Man, I got jumped last time, I'm not taking a chance on it happening again."

Matt nodded. "Yeah, man, I understand. You don't even look a hundred percent recovered yet. But...the thing is, Joey and Denny aren't around tonight. They're over in Estrella dealing."

"And Jenny didn't go with them?"

"No, I heard her say she was too wasted and needed to sleep the drugs off."

Once more Ross felt suspicious of Matt's true motives, but Matt's next words relaxed him: "I mean, after they left, I looked in the window and there she was passed out on the bed. I could have just grabbed her then and made off with her, but...well, I thought, what if the girl starts screaming and the cops come. I'm not family or anything...she could claim I was trying to rape her." He looked at Ross. "But you, you're family, and she being underage and all...so she can't make that much fuss. The neighbors call the police...well, you're her uncle, you're here to take her home. She'll have to go quietly." He shrugged. "Of course, she could run away again after you get her back home, but ..."

Ross nodded and got down off the hood of the car, then winced in pain. "Yeah, I get what you mean.

Let's get over there and pick up the little runaway. This has gone on for way, way too long."

Ross fished his car keys out of his pocket and handed them to Matt. "Hey, you drive. I'm not yet as recovered as I'd like to think I am."

"Yeah, sure thing," Matt replied with a cool smile.

They got into the car and set off.

CHAPTER 13

Joey's new hideaway was across town, on Tohono. This time it wasn't a trailer, but a suburban residence cut off from its neighbors by trees.

Using the cover of darkness to their advantage, Matt pulled off the road amidst a group of trees and parked. Ross felt satisfied that no one motoring past would notice the car.

Before getting out of the car, Ross pulled out his gun again and checked that the safety was off.

"No, no, no, man, put that away!" Matt instantly objected. "No guns."

Ross felt suspicious of Matt again. "But why? It's just for protection. Those punks are certain to be armed too."

Matt shook his head. "They aren't at home, man. And...guns are dangerous. You might wind up killing someone."

Ross looked very unconvinced. "Based on my last experience, you can't blame me for being less than willing to leave this firearm behind. I just don't want to go into that den of iniquity without some form of assurance that I'll make it out alive again."

"God is our protector," Matt said.

Ross frowned and stared at the firearm in his hand. "Yeah, when I prayed with Pastor Princeton this morning, he mentioned something about God sending angels to protect me."

"Psalm 91, verses 11 and 12," Matt said.

Ross nodded. "Hey, sure, man, I believed it back then and I still do. But...well, you gotta admit...it makes good theory, but in practice it stretches my new-found faith a little thin to expect that Almighty God is actually here right now in the car with us. Or that his angels are."

Matt laughed. "Oh, brother Ross, God's angels are always with us. Closer than we ever think."

Ross opened up the glove compartment and put the gun away.

"Here, take this instead."

Ross was surprised to see that Matt was handing him a small Bible. "What's this for?"

"Just a reminder that the Lord is with us in our quest tonight. Keep it in your pocket."

Ross took the Bible and put it away in his pocket. He looked out of the window towards Joey's house and suddenly felt impatient to get on with things. Still looking out of the window, he asked: "We can go now?"

Matt nodded. "Now is as good a time as ever."

The two of them made their way down the road to Joey's house.

"How'd the kid get this house on such short notice?" Ross asked Matt as they got closer to the large suburban bungalow. "This place seems quite expensive."

"As far as I can tell, they're illegal squatters. The owners of the place are out of town for a while and Joey and Denny just broke the back door and moved in. Of course, that means they've gotta be extra careful how they come and go, so as not to alert the neighbors to their presence."

They'd reached the house. There was no car parked out front and no lights on in front either.

"You're sure she's in here?" Ross asked Matt.

"Round the back. The master bedroom."

They walked round the house and before they'd turned the rear corner, Ross heard softly playing music. Then he saw light peeking through a set of shut drapes. They walked over to the window and peered in. Jennifer was sitting at the edge of the bed, brushing her hair with slow and mechanical motions that reminded Ross of a robot he'd once watched on TV. She was swaying to the pop music coming from a radio and showed no sign of realizing that she was being watched.

"Follow me," Matt whispered. "The back door's always open; they had to break it to use the place."

Ross did as he was told and he and Matt were soon inside the building and making their way over to the master bedroom.

***

"Hey, Jenny, it's time to go home," Ross said, once they were inside the bedroom.

Jennifer spun around in shock and gaped at him, her eyes dark pits in her fleshy face; the pit-like impression created by the dark eye makeup she had on. She looked wasted and smelt like she'd been vomiting again, though both her tee shirt and jeans were clean enough.

The bedroom however was as much a mess as the trailer they'd moved here from.

"Uncle Ross?" Jennifer finally asked, getting to her feet but still brushing her hair with a mechanical motion. "What are you doing here?"

"He's here to take you back home, Jenny," Matt replied before Ross could. "Your mother is very worried about you."

"Who're you?" Jennifer asked. "Some friend of Joey's? Hey, I'll tell him you snitched on him to my family and he'll murder you."

Ross sighed. "Stop it, kid. Matt here is the guy who rescued me after you and your drug dealer boyfriend left me tied up in the woods." He tried to look as tough as he could. "Now, listen here, we're here to take you back to your mom. So just get up and get packed and let's go before Joey and Denny come back. Yeah, and write them a note warning them not to come around to the house 'cos I'm living there now."

Jennifer put her hairbrush down. "I'm not going back there," she said coldly. "I'm not going back to mom's place. You can't make me go."

"Oh yes I can," Ross corrected her. "You're leaving here tonight."

"I'll scream," Jennifer threatened. "I'll start yelling the place down."

Ross shrugged. "Go on, start screaming. See if I care."

"You're underage and he's your uncle," Matt told her. "The police will take his side."

Jennifer glared at them both, the expression in her young-adult eyes that of a trapped animal. She seemed to be calculating whether or not she'd be able to make it past them and out through the door. To forestall her making the attempt, Matt adjusted his position so that his body was blocking the doorway. There was a bathroom door behind Jennifer, but she didn't appear to have thought of bolting through it. Or maybe the bathroom door didn't have a key.

"Well, what're you waiting for?" Ross barked at her in his regular tough-guy voice, which felt strangely unfamiliar to him now. "Hurry up and get packed, or we'll drag you along as you are."

Jennifer nodded coldly at him, then spat on the floor. "Okay, I'll get my things. But I don't know why the hell you're doing this to me. It ain't like you and mom ever see eye to eye on religion."

Ross smiled. "Let's just say that I've had a change of heart in a few areas."

Jennifer flung him a black look, then turned away and pulled out the nightstand beside her. She rifled through it for a few seconds, found something in there and turned back to face her uncle.

He groaned. She'd pulled a switchblade knife on them. The knife didn't really scare Ross—he'd been in his share of knife fights—but the look on Jennifer's face worried him. She looked crazed, crazed enough to hurt herself if she didn't get her way now.

"I'm not going back home with you guys and that's final," she moaned, waving the knife at them. "Hey, don't you dare come any closer than that," she whispered at Matt when he took a step towards her, then placed the knife against her own throat. "I'll kill myself if either of you two touch me."

Matt nodded and stepped back. "Yeah yeah, okay, girl."

"You can't kill yourself, Jenny," Ross said. "Suicide is a sin."

That statement stopped Jennifer in her tracks. "Huh, what did you just say?"

Ross nodded. "It's true, Jennifer. Suicide is a sin. Your body is the temple of God and if you destroy it, God will destroy you too." Ross had no idea where the words had come from. He wasn't even sure they were true—sure, suicide was a bad thing and not to be encouraged. But a sin?

Jennifer however, looked thunderstruck: "When did you start believing what the Bible said?"

Now Ross felt embarrassed. "Two nights ago? After you kids almost killed me. While lying there in the woods with my mouth taped shut, I had the realization that I was going to Hell and that was it. And I suspect the same thing applies to you if you kill yourself in your current ..." He didn't know the word for it and looked to Matt for help.

Matt smiled. "Backslidden state."

Ross returned his attention to Jennifer. "Yeah, if you kill yourself in a backslidden state you're certain to go to Hell too, and what's the point of that, knowing how much God loves you?"

Jennifer looked at him. "So, like, you're a Christian now, Uncle Ross? You're born again now, like Mom and like I used to be?"

Ross nodded, brought out his Bible and waved it at her. "Yes, I'm now saved by God's grace."

Jennifer stared from Ross to Matt. Then she lowered the knife from her throat and burst out laughing. "Hahahaha!" She flung the knife onto the bed, bent over and grabbed her belly and laughed and laughed and then pointed at Ross and kept on laughing. Ross wasn't certain about it because of her black makeup, but the teenager looked like she had tears in her eyes.

"What's so funny?" he asked.

Jennifer stopped laughing and sighed. "You are, Uncle Ross. I just can't believe that after I've escaped being conned by religion, you've gotten conned in my place. That's all. You used to be so cool. I used to envy you, how you were so independent and how my mom couldn't wrap you around her finger and order you around. But...How ridiculous can you get? You now believe in God and Jesus and all that nonsense?"

"You used to believe in it too. I remember you preaching to me."

She shrugged and slumped down onto the bed, and in that moment, reminded Ross of the way he remembered her before drugs wrecked her life. "Yeah, I guess I did believe it," she said. "Christianity made sense to me once. But since dad died everything's become so damn miserable and blurry. Going to church seemed like a chore, and then I met Joey and ..."

"Drugs seemed like the correct way to enlightenment, right?" Matt asked.

Jennifer nodded at him. "Well, at least Joey isn't judging me all the time like he's God, like mom does."

"Your mother loves you, Jenny," Ross said. "Try to understand that, okay? God loves you and your mom does too. I'll admit there's some things—like your dad's death—that make no real sense to me if God really does love you like he claims to, but I'm new to this Christianity thing and ..." He smiled. "Hey, how 'bout if you pack up your stuff and go home with me and we'll try to figure things out together? How 'bout we do that? Sure, your dad's no longer here with us, but you and me, we'll try to work things out together. How about that, Jenny?"

Ross saw that he'd gotten through to her, punched through her shell of teenaged indifference. "Yeah," Jennifer said, "I think I'd like that." She stared at him with a question in her young eyes, a plea and a hope that she could trust him. "You promise me that you'll hang around? You won't leave me alone with mom? Yeah, I know she cares about me and all that, but ..."

"Yeah, I'll hang around," Ross promised. "Don't you worry about that. We'll get you off the drugs and cleaned up and we'll both attend church together. Now just get your things together and let's go home and begin this new life as a family."

Jennifer smiled weakly at him. "Okay, Uncle Ross, I believe you. I'll get my stuff and I'll leave here with you."

"Oh no, she isn't going anywhere," a familiar voice said from the bedroom doorway.

"Hell no, she ain't," another high-pitched male voice added.

Ross groaned. He had no idea how Joey and Denny had caught them off guard. Except if...He looked around for Matt, but Matt was no longer in the bedroom with them. Ross remembered that Matt had been blocking off the bedroom door so that Jennifer couldn't flee through it, but where was he now?

Had Matt run off or, inconceivably, sold him out?

CHAPTER 14

At about the same time that Ross and Matt had begun talking to Jennifer, Samantha Wallace was suddenly struck by an intense compulsion to pray.

Ross had told her that he might be home late, so she wasn't bothered that he'd not called her yet, but now she suddenly felt that he was in grave danger. And, remembering where he'd told he was heading too—Joey's old home—only made Samantha more concerned.

She'd been watching television, but the burden to pray felt so heavy that she turned off the TV and got down on her knees beside the couch.

"Heavenly Father," she prayed. "Please help my brother Ross find Jenny. Please help and protect him wherever he is. Please send your angels to keep him safe....and please, Father, please protect my little girl Jennifer too. You know she doesn't really mean to cause you all this bother ..."

CHAPTER 15

"No, Jenny isn't goin' anywhere with you, old man," Joey said, shouldering his way past Ross till he was standing beside the girl, though Denny remained by the bedroom door, as if he was trying to stop Ross from retreating.

Both young men were pointing guns at Ross.

Joey pulled Jennifer up to stand beside him. "Old man, my girl wants to remain here with her man, where it's nice and easy and the high never ends." He kissed Jennifer's purple hair. "Don't you, baby?"

"Yeah, I guess so," Jennifer replied, staring guiltily at her uncle.

Joey shrugged at Ross. "See? The girl loves me."

Ross frowned. Joey's face was once more wild from cocaine usage and maybe some uppers too. Once again, he was bouncing on his feet like he was having trouble standing still.

"Hear that, Uncle Ross?" Denny said in a mocking imitation of Jenny's voice. "Your niece don't wanna leave her loving boyfriend. She don't wanna go back there and be holy-rolled on again by her religious fanatic of a mom."

Jennifer was giggling now as if amused, as if she'd quickly repented of her initial repentance.

Ross groaned, again wondering where Matt had departed to on such short notice. He just hoped the guy would hear the noise and come back quickly.

"For God's sake, guys, let the girl go home with me, okay? She's still underage, too young to be living with you two and getting stoned all the time."

"Man, you must be hard of hearing," Joey said, a wicked look now coming over his face. "I already told you she's remaining here with us."

"Yeah," Denny agreed, stepping forward and placing the muzzle of his gun against Ross's left ear. "Maybe I kicked you too hard in the head last time and scrambled your brains. Maybe you need another hard thump to the head to settle your brains down right again, so you realize we ain't kidding with you."

"We should've just killed you two nights ago in the woods," Joey said. "Then you won't be here now giving us this nonsense."

Denny shoved Ross forward. "Still time to rectify that tho'. We don't live here, the house owners are out of town for a month, so if we shoot you, no need to even dispose of the body. You'd have rotted away before their return."

"No, Denny, we're not going to shoot him," Jennifer said. "We've already been over that." Then her expression turned confused, as if she'd just remembered something, and she stared at Ross. "Hey, Uncle Ross, where'd your friend go?" she asked.

"I think he ran off and left me," Ross said gloomily.

"What friend?" Joey asked with a suspicious and worried look in his eyes. "Who're you talking about, baby?"

"There was another guy with Uncle Ross, standing by the bedroom door," Jennifer explained, making

Ross wince at her betrayal. "His name's Matt. He's a tall guy, almost as big as Denny, wearing a 'Jesus Saves' tee shirt."

"Who's he? One of your mom's friends?"

Jennifer shook her head. "No, never seen him before, but I think he's from mom's church."

"I'll go check the house for him," Denny said and left.

Ross felt better with Denny out of the way. Having that big and likely unstable young man behind him was unsettling.

"Now look, Joey," he said, the words out of his mouth before he could stop himself, "You need to give your life to Christ. You need to accept Jesus as your Lord and personal savior and stop messing kids' lives up with the drugs you're dealing."

"Huh?" Joey looked confused, then stared at Jennifer. "I thought your uncle was a tough guy, when did he get religion?"

Jennifer laughed. "Two nights ago, after we kicked the living daylights out of him."

Joey looked coldly at Ross. "And so, now that you've seen the light, you think it's your God-given calling to save sinners like me, right?"

Ross ignored the anger in the young man's voice. "For God so loved the world that he gave his only begotten son, that whosoever shalt believe in him should not perish, but have everlasting life." He smiled. "I think I quoted that right—I've heard Jenny's mom say it to me enough times."

Joey was not amused. "Screw you, old man."

Ross shrugged. "Joey, in my book you most definitely qualify as a sinner. Kid, you need to give up the drug life and give your life to Jesus."

Joey looked down at Jennifer. "Is this guy for real?"

She nodded. "Yeah. He was holy-rolling me before you and Denny returned."

Joey turned back to Ross and now there was murder in his eyes. "Alright, I've had enough of this nonsense. Let's get things clear and straight right now, okay? Jenny is staying here with me. You just run on home to her momma and say you didn't find her."

"I'm sorry I can't do that," Ross said. "I promised Sam that I'd bring her back and that's what I intend to do."

Joey took a step forward and placed the muzzle of his gun against Ross's forehead. "And how do you intend to do that, huh?"

"Joey, please, don't shoot him!" Jennifer protested.

Ross however felt no fear. This time was different from last time. The last time he'd found himself in this situation, he'd had no hope, all that had awaited him after death had been a blackness and an eternity of torment. Now, however, he knew deep in his heart that he was Heaven-bound. No, he didn't want to die, but death no longer bore the terror for him that it once had.

He said nothing, but Joey clearly saw the peace in his eyes, because he laughed. "Well, if you're that ready to go to Heaven, maybe I'll just help you along."

"Don't kill me, Joey," Ross said calmly. "It's a sin to kill someone."

"Baby, don't," Jennifer pleaded.

"Stay out of this, girl," Joey retorted. "If this uncle of yours won't keep his nose out of our business voluntarily, maybe we'll just have to help him, right?"

"Hey, how about if I just go home with him, huh?" Jennifer said.

Still keeping the gun pressed against Ross's head, Joey spun around to stare at her. "What? You wanna leave me and go back home?"

She nodded. "Yeah, I'll be sixteen in two months anyway, and then if I leave home no one can stop me. And then I'll come right back here."

"I don't like it," Joey said. "This uncle of yours knows too much about my business and—"

He was interrupted by Denny's arrival at the bedroom door. Denny was eating a sandwich and was pushing Matt ahead of him. "Hey, I found this guy in the kitchen—"

But the distraction—because Joey was so surprised to see Matt that he instantly took all his attention off of Ross—allowed Ross to slip his head away from the gun placed against it and also to disarm Joey. Joey turned from staring at Matt in surprise, to staring at Ross in surprise.

"Damn it," Denny said, "he's got your gun."

Ross had only taken away the gun to protect himself, in case Joey forgot himself and accidentally pulled the trigger. He didn't intend to shoot at anyone, but Denny clearly thought he did.

Because the next thing that happened, Denny fired at him twice.

Both bullets hit Ross; one in the chest, one in the belly.

Oh, God, please no, he thought as he sank to the ground, the gun slipping from his fingers. But this time he didn't feel any fear, instead, as the pain came and he felt himself blacking out, he felt a deep assurance that if he died tonight it would have been worth it.

CHAPTER 16

"What have you done, you idiot?" Jennifer screamed at Denny as she rushed to her uncle's side. "We were just discussing that I'd go home with him and come back in two months when I'm older!"

"He took Joey's gun!" Denny protested. "He was gonna shoot us!"

Jennifer knelt by Ross's side. "Uncle Ross! Uncle Ross! I'm sorry! I'm sorry!"

Ross coughed up a trickle of blood. "It's okay. At least I'm saved now. I'm going to Heaven."

"Hey, guys, he can still survive this," Matt said. "Just call an ambulance. You guys can leave. I'll stay here with him till the ambulance arrives. I won't say a word about what really happened. I'll just say I was walking past the house and heard gunshots and came in here and—"

"You're lying," Joey said. "I can see it in your eyes. You holy rollers are addicted to telling the truth, so, once we've gone the cops will soon be combing everywhere looking for us."

"So what we gonna do now then?" Denny asked. He'd begun breaking out in a cold sweat.

"We clean up the evidence of the crime," Joey said, bending over and picking up his gun from where Ross had dropped it. With a cruel smile on his lips he pointed over at Ross, who was still breathing, but was unconscious with blood bubbling from his lips. "No evidence equals no arrests and no convictions."

"What are you talking about?" Jennifer asked nervously. "Matt is right. Let's just call an ambulance. I can even claim that I shot him, but let's call 911."

"Sorry, honey," Joey said, aiming the gun at her. "I really hate to have to do this, but I think our beautiful romance just ended. The way I see it, if you three are dead, then no one can link either Denny or I to your uncle's death."

Tears filled Jennifer's eyes. "You're gonna kill me? Joey, you said you loved me!"

"Honey, love's just a four-letter word. If you really wanted to be loved, you should've stayed with Jesus. He's into all that love nonsense. Me, I'm just trying to satisfy my sexual needs and make a few dollars."

Joey laughed at her, then gestured to Denny. "Hey, bring that one in here and place him beside her. Kill 'em both at once. That way there's less chance of the gunshot noise being reported."

"Hey, don't do this man!" Matt protested as he was shoved towards Ross and Jennifer. "You're making a big mistake."

"Dude, shut up and move," Denny said, prodding him in the back with his gun. "The big mistake was you two sticking your noses in our business."

Joey smirked at Matt. "Yeah, and when you get to Heaven, say 'Hi' to Jesus for us."

"You can't do this to us," Jennifer protested, tears filling her blue eyes.

Joey laughed and pointed the gun at her. "Baby, just say your last prayers."

CHAPTER 17

Jennifer stared at the gun. All she could think of was that she'd made the worst mistake of her young life leaving her mother and hooking up with Joey Crockett, who'd just revealed himself to be a bastard of the worst sort. He'd told her he loved her, and she'd believed him. And he'd only been using her. The betrayal stung her and suddenly she felt like crying.

She looked down at Uncle Ross. He looked like he was still alive, but his eyes were closed and the pool of blood around him seemed to be widening. And he was dying because he'd actually cared about her; had risked his life twice now to rescue her from Joey; but she'd been too blind to see that he really meant well.

"Oh, God, please help me now!" she pleaded silently, unable to look at the gun in Joey's hands. She could hear Denny sniggering though, clearly amused by the silent and desperate motions of her lips. "If you save me now, I'll be a good girl," she prayed. "I promise to be real good. I'll stop sinning and attend church, and love my mom, and do everything the Bible says I should. But please save me...no, save us—all three of us."

"Okay, I think that's about enough praying," Joey said with a laugh. "I'm not sure why I even asked you to pray. Seeing as you're about meeting Jesus, you'll soon be talking to him in person."

"Okay, you two, this has gone far enough," Matt said, in a tone of voice that made Jennifer turn and stare at him. His voice now sounded authoritative; not scared at all.

Denny, who had his gun trained on Matt, smirked at him. "And what are you gonna do about it? Come back as a ghost and report us to the cops?"

"Goodbye, Jenny," Joey said.

"No don't!" Jennifer shrieked.

But Joey pulled the trigger anyway.

And then the impossible happened and time seemed to slow down. The reason why Jennifer got this impression was because two things happened at once and she saw them both happen, but they all happened so fast—and *after* Joey fired at her—that there was honestly no way she could have witnessed them happening in real time.

This was the impossible reality you experienced but still didn't really believe.

First of all, Matt changed. From a normal-sized guy, he was suddenly about seven feet tall. In addition to which his clothes altered to some kind of Roman-empire-era garb—toga and leather sandals...and he now had wings, large golden wings.

The second and craziest thing was that Matt *caught* the bullets that Joey had shot at Jennifer. And why she knew time had slowed down was because she actually saw 'Matt' catch the bullets—saw the slugs leave the muzzle of the gun; saw them in mid-air, heading for her face and she with no possible means of escape...and then suddenly Matt's right hand was there in front of her head and the bullets hit his right palm with loud thuds and his fingers closed around them ...

And time normalized again.

Jenny was too shocked for words. The phrase "He's an angel! He's an angel! He's an angel!" kept reverberating in her mind as she watched everything that happened next.

Matt the angel stepped in front of her to protect her, and he was so big that to actually see Denny and Joey now she had to peer around him, parting the lower golden feathers of his left wing with her fingers.

Joey and Denny were staring in shock.

"Who-who-who the heck are y-y-you?" Joey asked. He looked like he'd shoot the angel. Denny was trembling with fear, his mouth agape, and looked like he was being electrocuted. Jennifer was amused by the sight.

Once more time seemed frozen; this time by Joey and Denny's indecision. It was obvious that what they'd just witnessed was so far out of left field that they had no idea how to respond to it.

"Go," Matt told Joey and Denny. "You may go to Heaven or you may go to Hell. The choice is entirely yours."

That broke the deadlock. In seconds both Joey and Denny had fled the bedroom and Jennifer heard them scrambling along the hallway, bursting out of the back door and running around the rear of the house.

Matt turned to her.

Wow, she thought. *Is this what an angel looks like?* His face and clothes all glowed with brilliant light; and there was a sense of majesty about him. She felt wrapped up in his aura, caught up in a sensation of holiness in which the world around her paled into insignificance. Jennifer could sense the angel's power; it was indescribable; looking at 'Matt,' she just knew he was an angelic being, representing the universe's ultimate ruler.

No wonder Joey and Denny ran like scared rabbits, she thought. *No way, I'd wanna mess with this guy. I'd run like hell too if he wasn't on my side.*

From the front of the house, Jennifer heard a car start up and pull out into the road with screeching tires.

She laughed, but then instantly sobered when she saw that the angel was staring down at her.

"I'm your guardian angel, Jennifer Wallace," he told her solemnly. "And you've caused me a huge amount of trouble. I think it's about time you returned home and behaved yourself like a Christian girl should. Don't you?"

She nodded. "Yeah, sure ..." she began saying, but then remembered her wounded uncle and spun around to look at him instead. "Oh my God, Uncle Ross! Noooo!" She knelt and shook him, trying to revive him, then turned to the angel. "Please do something! He's dying!"

Matt smiled down at her. "Don't worry, Jennifer. Ross Blakely will live. Almighty God has already decreed that he will survive this, because God has a great work he needs him for. But we must get him to a hospital. Where is your cellphone?"

Jennifer hurried over and got her cellphone from her purse and dialed 911.

"Hello, I'd like to report a shooting ..."

When she turned around after giving the 911 operator the house address, Matt the angel was gone.

With a smile on her face, Jennifer hurried over and sat beside her wounded uncle and waited for the ambulance to arrive.

He caught the bullets, she remembered in amazement. *My guardian angel can actually catch bullets. He's faster than Superman!*

CHAPTER 18

Two Months Later

Ross, Samantha and Jennifer all sat in the front pew of the Joy of Life Bible Church on a warm Sunday morning while Pastor Princeton preached a sermon on the Prodigal Son.

"Or in this case, the Prodigal *Daughter*," Ross whispered to Jennifer, who giggled. This was two months after the shooting incident at the house and Ross was mostly recovered now. He also now lived permanently with Samantha and Jennifer, who once more looked like the decent Christian young lady she'd been before she had her 'dark experience' as her mother called it.

"... And so, my dear brothers and sisters in the lord," Pastor Princeton was saying," never forget that, just like the love of the father in the tale of the Prodigal Son, so also Jesus's love for us is boundless. He is truly the good shepherd, who lays down His life for his sheep." Then, smiling down at Jennifer, he added, "And if even just one little lamb gets lost and wanders astray, Jesus does His utmost best to restore he or she to the fold."

Tears of joy in her eyes, Samantha hugged Jennifer tightly to her. "Yes, honey, God really did restore you to me!"

While the congregation applauded, Jennifer began weeping too.

Ross smiled. He knew this scripture applied to him too. He'd been lost and was now found. And he was grateful that God had taken the time to seek him out and save him, both from sin and Hell, and also to save his life, not once, but twice.

***

Joey Crockett and Denny were still in hiding, with the police looking for them.

***

No one had seen Matt since the night that Ross got shot. And from what Jennifer had told her uncle, her mother and her pastor, none of them expected to ever see him again.

The End.

ABOUT THE AUTHOR

Gary Lee Vincent was born in Clarksburg, West Virginia and is an accomplished author, musician, actor, producer, director and entrepreneur. In 2010, his horror novel *Darkened Hills* was selected as 2010 Book of the Year winner by *Foreword Reviews Magazine* and became the pilot novel for *DARKENED - THE WEST VIRGINIA VAMPIRE SERIES*, that encompasses the novels *Darkened Hills, Darkened Hollows, Darkened Waters, Darkened Souls, Darkened Minds* and *Darkened Destinies.* He has also authored the bizarro thriller *Passageway,* a tribute to H.P. Lovecraft.

Gary co-authored the novel *Belly Timber* with John Russo, Solon Tsangaras, Dustin Kay and Ken Wallace, and co-authored the novel *Attack of the Melonheads* with Bob Gray and Solon Tsangaras.

As an actor, Gary has appeared in over seventy feature films and multiple television series, including *House of Cards*, *Mindhunter*, *The Walking Dead*, and *Stranger Things*.

As a director, Gary got his directorial debut with *A Promise to Astrid.* He has also directed the films *Desk Clerk*, *Dispatched*, *Godsend* and the 2020 remake of John Russo's iconic horror film *Midnight.*

Made in the USA
Columbia, SC
19 January 2021

31236435R00052